Acknowledgment
The publishers would like to thank John Dillow
for the cover illustration.

Ladybird books are widely available, but in case of
difficulty may be ordered by post or telephone from:

Ladybird Books – Cash Sales Department
Littlegate Road Paignton Devon TQ3 3BE
Telephone 0803 554761

A catalogue record for this book is available
from the British Library

Published by Ladybird Books Ltd Loughborough Leicestershire UK
Ladybird Books Inc Auburn Maine 04210 USA

About the
farm

by JACQUELINE HARDING
illustrated by SARA SLIWINSKA

Ladybird

The animals on the farm are waking up.

animals

The hens have laid some lovely brown eggs.

hens

The sheep are looking for some long, juicy grass to eat.

sheep

The pigs are eating
from the trough.
Pigs eat anything!

pigs

The horse is not in her stable. She's galloping in the field.

horse

The cows are being milked in the cowshed. The tanker has come to collect all the milk.

COWS

Goats give milk, too.
This goat has chewed
the farmer's hat!

goat

A combine harvester has been busy in the field.

combine harvester

A sheepdog looks after the sheep. He found some that were lost.

sheepdog

The mother cat is
in the barn with
her kittens.

cat kittens

The tractor is bringing
the bales of hay from
the field.

tractor **hay**

Every day on a farm
is very busy.
Good night!

farm